MAGUS the LOLLIPOP MAN

Michael Mullen
Illustrated by Harry Horse

WOLFHOUND PRESS / CANONGATE

Paperback edition 1983

First published 1981 by Canongate Publishing, Edinburgh.

Published in Ireland by
WOLFHOUND PRESS
68 Mountjoy Square, Dublin 1.

British Library Cataloguing in Publication Data
Mullen, Michael
Magus, the lollipop man.
I. Title
823'.914[J] PZ7

ISBN 0-86327-017-4 (Wolfhound Press)
ISBN 0-86241-054-1 (Canongate Publishing)

Michael Mullen works as a teacher in his native County Mayo.
Harry Horse is an illustrator living and working in Edinburgh.
Front cover design: Jim Hutcheson
Cover illustrations: Harry Horse

This book is published with the assistance of
The Arts Council (An Chomhairle Ealaíon),
Dublin, Ireland.

Typeset in Scotland by
Hewer Text Composition Services, Edinburgh.
Printed and bound in Great Britain by
Billing and Sons Limited Worcester.

To my wife, Deirdre

1

Magus the lollipop man came down the hill and stood on the bridge one summer morning. From the bridge he could see the town of Hornbottom. The sun was pink and half hot. Its rays caught the dew drops on the grass blades and filled them with silver. On the trees the leaves were full and green and cool. And the pink light was getting in everywhere. It floated over window sills and lit up all the dark corners of rooms. It was going to be a hot day but it was not as yet hot.

The lollipop man was a fat man. He had a large floppy hat and the wide brim cast a shadow on his eyes. He had a very large coat which was more like a cloak. It was twice too big for a man but for the lollipop man it was just right. It had a foot-and-a-half deep pockets and they were all stuffed with lollipops.

He stood on the humped back bridge which had been built a long time ago and listened to the waters rush over the rocks a little up-stream. It was a soft sound like a hush which wanted the world to listen. He listened. He could hear the song of the birds from the trees and the bushes and the shrubs. The sound was everywhere and it filled his ears.

Magus the lollipop man looked at the town. It was not a large town, just large enough for a lollipop man to set his lollipops before the children were awake in the green lawns which had been carefully cut until they looked like carpets. His lollipops were just a little taller than the cut grass and there they could shine in the sun. Lollipops were never planted in fields.

The village clock had a solemn face. It had been solemn for two hundred years and its twelve figures and two hands were very large. It was coming up to seven o'clock. The bells rang out. They rang out eight times for seven hours and the lollipop man knew that the vicar was a sensible man. Nobody else in the world had a clock which rang eight times when the small hand showed up at seven. He wondered if the bells rang once or thirteen times when the small hand reached twelve.

He milked his long white beard. He always milked his long white beard when he was deciding upon something. He had decided on where to begin planting lollipops. He made his way to the Yellow Tavern which had its blinds down like large eyelids. He plunged his hand deep into his pockets and took out a handful of lollipops. There were yellow lollipops and green lollipops and blue lollipops and red lollipops and many other coloured lollipops.

"Aha," he said with a long "aah", "I will start planting lollipops here. I will plant all sorts of coloured lollipops for Barney Perkins for something tells me, which tells me everything, that Barney Perkins is not just feeling himself at this very moment."

Barney Perkins had not been feeling himself for a long time now and Mister and Missus Perkins were very worried about him. For no reason at all he had taken ill. He became very thin and Doctor Pink had poked at him and examined him and mused about him and could find nothing wrong with him. But that did no good for Barney Perkins. He wasted away in the big room above the tavern and Missus Perkins who was very fat and full was worried. He refused his breakfast and he refused his dinner and he refused everything which was brought to him and lots of things had been brought to him. He lay in his bed very weak, his head deep in large pillows and he only moved his large blue eyes.

"Coloured lollipops for Master Perkins," the lollipop man said, selecting lollipops from the handful of lollipops he held before him. He selected them carefully and put the rest of them back into his deep pockets. Then moving about the lawn briskly he planted a circle of coloured lollipops with the initials BP in the middle, which stood for Barney Perkins, and went on his way.

He stopped by another garden and looked at the lawn. It was a sad, badly cut lawn and the grass was thick and tufted and falling to one side. He looked at the house. It certainly needed a new coat of paint and the pink sun cheered it up only a little. The paint on the door had blistered here and there and the weather board was held on one hinge so that it scraped every time the door was opened. Yes, the lollipop man knew all about it. "This is little George Wallace's house. He is the orphan who stays with Missus Tucker. Why, little George Wallace hasn't had a lollipop since way back before Christmas and Missus Tucker treats George very badly. Nobody likes George Wallace or his little dog."

He plunged his hand deep into his pocket and fetched out the very largest lollipop he had. It must have been as large as a dinner plate and thick as a thumb and it would require a whole night and a whole day of tongue-licking just to wear it half thin. It was the best lollipop he had and it had taken him a whole week to mix its colours. He pushed the stem into the ground and then straightened his stiff back to look at it. It looked like the sun coming up out of the sea in the green grass which was falling to one side.

He bent down again, his old bones creaking and placed small lollipops around the large one. "Yes," he said to himself, "Little George Wallace will be pleased with his lollipops. Just wait until he sees them. Why, his face will just light up!" And having said that he was on his way again.

He made his way down the street, his large coat gathered about him and his large brimmed hat flopping over his ears and his eyes. The sun was getting warmer and the shadows thrown by the houses shorter. Summer sun is good for a lollipop man's back. It warms him up and dries out the dew which comes up at night from the ground when he is sleeping by the hedgerows.

He worked during the winter in his little cottage boiling sugars and mixing in colours and tastes from large bottles which he kept on his shelves. Nobody knew how to mix colours and tastes except a proper lollipop man. It was an old secret he had learned from an old lollipop man when he was very young. He had learned which berries to crush into juice in his press which was made with wood from the mast of a Spanish galleon he had found on the coast of Cornwall. Of course it took time to learn how to know good berries from bad ones and a wet summer with little sun always made him sad. He knew then that the juice would be poor and thin and the lollipops themselves without lustre. Last year had been good for lollipops.

The milkman, Councillor Bitterberry, came by on his float and gave him a quizzical eye. Strangers were never welcome in Hornbottom, particularly ones with deep pockets. One never knew what they were up to between stealing hens and vegetables and making off with eggs. The rattle of the wheels on the cobblestones made a racket which disturbed the quiet corners of the town.

Magus found more lawns and planted more lollipops. He looked about at his morning's work and a broad smile spread over his face. He had certainly brightened up the town. He felt very satisfied with himself. He turned and made his way down to the river. He would sleep there under the trees and listen to the water passing by and later in the day he would steep his tired feet. They were very sore and very red for he had walked a long way during the night and had only taken a short rest on the way. He always had to have his work finished very early in the morning. A lollipop man must never be caught growing lollipops. That was the first rule.

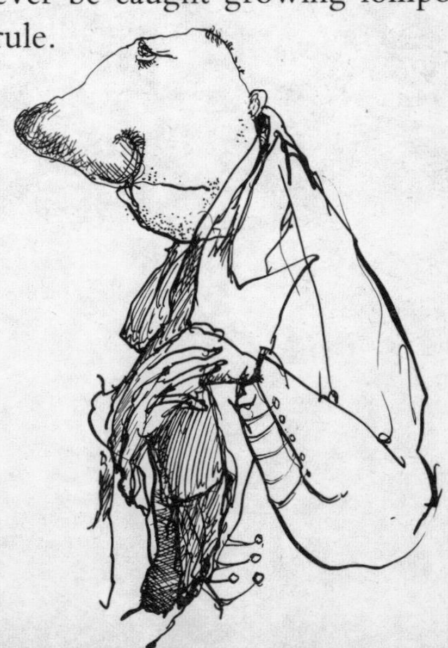

2

The town of Hornbottom was a small English town. It was very old in parts and even the new houses seemed older than they were. Squire Wickle and the councillors did not welcome strangers to Hornbottom and gave them a look which suggested that they should move on. It had been like that for a very long time, ever since the stranger brought the plague way back in 1800.

"We will have no truck with strangers," Councillor Dobson the butcher often said. He always had his butcher's boater hat on and a long steel rasp at his side on which he sharpened his knives. "Brought the plague before and will bring it again. And if they don't bring the plague, well, you just don't know what they are going to bring. Don't mind country folks coming to the town but strangers are a different matter."

And so said all the tradesman in the town when they sat about the dark oak table in the dark panelled oak room with Squire Wickle on his large oak throne. He had a red face which was pitted here and there, a purple nose and a tweedy moustache. None of the children of the town liked to look at his face for very long or at his nose which was purple.

"Cost Squire Wickle a lot of money to bring up the purple on that large nose of his," the mothers often said to the children but they could not for the life of them see why he should spend so much money bringing up the purple in his nose.

He lived at Wickle Hall, a house with large brick gables and chimneys and mysterious cellars. The large brick house set among trees had its own ghost. Squire Wickle did not mind ghosts. Every old house boasted a ghost but he disliked intensely the ghost at Wickle Hall because it was large and jolly and laughed uproariously. It had been silent only once, and that in amazement, when the Squire had tittered for some reason or other twenty years previously.

Sometimes, a little after midnight, when Squire Wickle was having his toddy in front of a warm fire, the ghost came and sat in the large armchair opposite him and asked him riddles which he could never answer. And when Squire Wickle could not answer them the ghost would give the answer and fall off the armchair with laughter and roll about on the carpet. Squire Wickle did not like this at all. He looked up the family records which went back a long way and discovered that the ghost had been court jester to the king.

He had spent a winter in the Tower of London for telling his jokes. The king had laughed so heartily at some of his remarks during a feast that he fell from his throne and broke a leg. His councillors said that the jester was a Spanish plot. They proved their point by showing that the jester told his best jokes when the king's mouth was full in order that the king might choke in his laughter. For this he was lodged in the tower and a sentence passed that he should be hanged, drawn and quartered. But in his absence the king became very serious and it came hard on the councillors of the palace to please him so they had to discount the plot and restore the jester to his rightful place at the feet of the king. For his services to the king he had been given lands in the country and a country house. Squire Wickle, his direct descendant, now occupied that country house.

"Why, by my shin bones and by my jester shoe bells but you are a very serious fellow, just like those councillors who had me lodged in the tower for making the king laugh. Not a Wickle at all. I'm very ashamed of you. Don't know why you never want people to be happy. Why, you just seem to hate people being happy. Some sour drop in you somewhere."

"Enough of your prattle," the Squire told him, "life is a very serious business."

"No, it is not. There is no law which tells us we should not be happy. You give me the page and paragraph."

"It is implied. Never knew a judge who was happy."

"That's why they hang folks."

"They don't. Not any more."

"They would, given half a chance. Wished me hanged, drawn and quartered once. Why, I saw the hanging orders on parchment waiting for the king's seal."

They broke their conversation for a while and then the Squire turned to another subject.

"Are you going to haunt me always? Last night at three o'clock I heard you rolling about in the main hall laughing."

"I thought of a new pun. Do you wish to hear it?"

"No, I have no wish to hear your pun."

"The king would if he were still alive."

"Why can't you be like other ghosts? They are all very serious and thin. They are acceptable ghosts and very easy to live with."

"Do you know why they are serious."

"No."

"Because they have done evil deeds in their day. Why, I would not be seen in their company or allow myself to be driven in their ghostly coaches. Every ghost for miles around has something on his mind which is always bothering him. Only one ghost I ever liked very much and that was the ghost of Merton Hall. He was the ghost of a jolly monk who died from eating too much."

"What happened to him?"

"Well, when I met him first he was a very fat ghost. He had to come back to Merton Hall whenever they had a feast. He was obliged to look on at the feast from beginning to end. For four hundred years he had to return to Merton Hall until he had become thin. Watched the weight fall off him year by year until he was just ghostly skin and bones. Last time I met him he was just a shadow of himself. He had finished his haunting and made up for his misdemeanours."

Squire Wickle looked at the ghost with a sly eye.

"So, ghosts do not haunt houses forever?"

"No. Every ghost has a purpose in a house."

"What is your purpose?"

"Can't tell you that. I like it here. But you will know when my time is up."

"How will I know?"

"You will know," he said and left it at that.

The heat was getting to the ghost of Wickle Hall. He began to snore beside the log fire. Soon his snores were filling the room and his huge stomach was rising and falling to the snore. When he was fully asleep he melted away and all that Squire Wickle could hear were deep

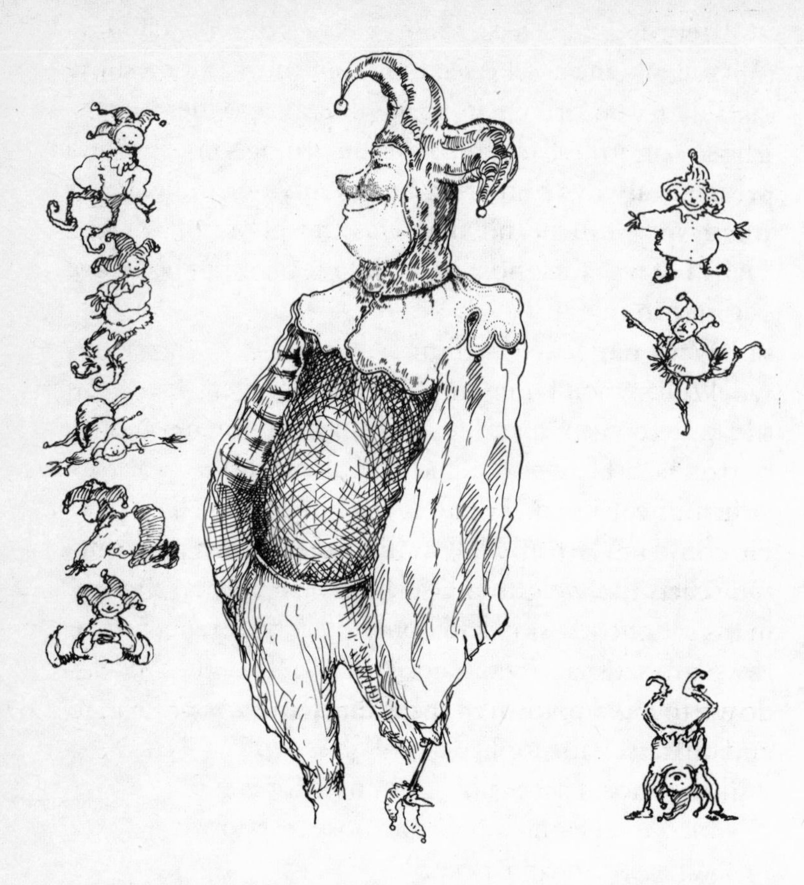

invisible snores and deep chuckles as the ghost remembered some pun or other from way back when he was still sitting at the king's feet in London.

The Squire was happy when the ghost fell asleep. He was a constant embarrassment to him. Ghost hunters from all over the country had written to Squire Wickle about him. Some even suggested that he might be a laughing ghost of which there were very few in England. He never answered their letters and he set his dogs on snoopers.

But his greatest fear was that people might discover the secret of the cellars. He could not endure this disclosure. His power would be weakened if not totally destroyed. There was nothing he liked better than to preside over the council meetings in the town hall. He was respected among the councillors. His "Ums" and "Ahs" as he sat in his large oak throne and let his mind cogitate on some trivial matter or other gave him great satisfaction. And he liked time to stand still. The whole world was changing too rapidly and not changing for the better. He would stay the march of time in Hornbottom as long as he could.

Just as well that ghosts disappeared during the day. He could never really discover where they went to, but they certainly went somewhere. Each morning, dressed in his tweeds and his plusfours, he would come through the great iron gates of Wickle Hall and make his way down to Hornbottom to check that there was no change and that today was like yesterday. He had to keep a vigilant eye on things.

3

But in the town of Hornbottom, today would never be like yesterday try as hard as Squire Wickle would try. Already the sun which had been cool and pink had turned a bright nine o' clock silver. While Magus the lollipop man rested down by the river with his fingers locked together over his broad stomach in contentment, the children of Hornbottom were waking up to the fact that lollipops were growing in front gardens.

Missus Perkins of the Yellow Tavern knuckled sleep out of her eyes and let the window blinds up so that the sun could pour into Master Barney Perkins' room. She yawned a deep wide yawn and looked down on the lawn fronting the Yellow Tavern.

"Oh my, Oh my!" she said when she saw the lollipops popping their heads over the lawn. "Why, somebody came this morning and planted lollipops all over the place. Oh master Barney but you should see all the lollipops in our front lawn. Never seen the likes of it in my life."

"Lollipops mother?" Barney Perkins said from his bed in a weak voice.

"Yes Master Barney. Neat and exact as toadstools."

"Let me see!"

"No. You may not see. You just stay under your warm blankets. Doctor Pink said that you must not move."

"But I've got to see them mother."

"Now don't you move. Remember what Doctor Pink said."

But he had begun to move. He pushed aside the sheets and the blankets and put his feet into his red slippers which were always and ever beside his bed. His legs were so thin that his mother thought he would fall on the floor. But he slid his feet into his red slippers, balanced himself and made his way over to the window. He looked down onto the lawn. It was like a sky full of different coloured stars. His eyes were filled with the sight of blue lollipops and green lollipops and lollipops of mixed colour and right in the middle were flaming red lollipops carrying his initials.

"Why, somebody wrote my initials in lollipops! I'm going straight down and getting some."

"Now don't you dare go down the stairs Master Barney Perkins. Remember that Doctor Pink said you would not be able to leave your bed for six more months."

"Don't care what Doctor Pink says," he told her, already on his way out of the door and down the tavern stairs which were very old. They creaked a lot and woke the Yellow Tavern keeper, Mister Perkins. He came to the door in his night gown, a cobweb of sleep in his eyes.

"What's this. What's this?" he said, not certain what was happening at so early an hour. He saw master Barney Perkins making his way painfully down the stairs.

"Missus Perkins," he called "young master Barney should be back in his bed. Doctor Pink said so. No knowing what chill he might pick up."

"I told him to come back to bed. But he wants to have some of those lollipops on the lawn."

"What lollipops?"

"The lollipops which appeared this morning."

"Lollipops don't appear in the morning."

"Well they *have* appeared *this* morning."

He followed the painful steps of Barney Perkins down the stairs.

Barney Perkins' eyes filled with delight when he looked at the the pattern of lollipops in the lawn. For a moment he stood still in wonder. Then he picked the first lollipop from the top of the letter B and began to suck it. It was the best lollipop he had ever tasted. It was like a bowl of strawberries crushed together and the juice strained straight into a lollipop.

"Why, this is the best lollipop I ever tasted," he said, his lips and chin all red from licking.

Missus Perkins could swear that it was from that moment that Master Barney Perkins began to draw up from his decline. He licked and licked until he was finished and then he picked another lollipop from the letter B and commenced to lick it.

"More here than meets the eye Mister Perkins," Missus Perkins said observing everything from the tavern door. "Now you go right back into bed and you don't say one word to nobody," she ordered her husband. Still half asleep and full of wonder he made his way back to the four poster bed on which King Henry had slept on his way through Hornbottom.

Meanwhile Master Barney Perkins was quite content in himself licking his third lollipop. The sun was shining on his pale white face and Missus Perkins could swear that his cheeks were becoming red from sucking on all the lollipops.

"Oh my, oh my, but what should I do?" she kept muttering to herself. She had never seen anything quite like it in all her life.

Little George Wallace had been cold the whole night through. It was always cold up in the attic under his threadbare blankets. Strange thing about little George Wallace was that he was always dreaming about food when he slept. He slept in a quite miserable triangular attic and the timber beams touched his head when he stood up. He gave a long yawn and peeped out from under the threadbare sheets. His small dog Boxer, an orphan like himself had one eye awake and was looking up at his master.

"Had a good night Boxer?" he called to the dog.

The dog did not blink his eye and he knew that the dog had been as cold as he. He wished to slip down between the sheets but Missus Tucker was calling him.

"You hurry down here George Wallace and eat your breakfast good and quick and be on your way to school."

He did not particularly wish to go to school. He was always bad at his lessons. He blotched his copy books. He could never get his spellings right and he preferred to walk down by the river with his dog Boxer and look at things. There was no particular thing at which he looked. He just looked at everything down by the river. He always felt particualry happy there and he could see no reason why he should go to school. He was also ashamed of going to school. His clothes were poor and he never had cheese or meat between his sandwiches like the others. And everybody kept away from little George Wallace. He was very little and there was a story around the school that nobody knew where he came from. So most of the day he was by himself in the bottom desk of the classroom or standing in a corner with a dunce's hat on his head. At playtime he sat by himself at the school railings and Boxer always came and put his two front pawns on the low coping and he patted his head. He was not permitted to bring Boxer into the school yard. Because they did not like Little George Wallace they did like not his dog either.

Little George Wallace cleaned his neck and his face and behind his ears and brushed his teeth. The water in the basin was very cold and there was only a small patch of sunshine in the small room. By midday the patch of sunshine would have travelled across the floor and up the wall and by one o' clock the room would be grey and cold again. Little George Wallace loved the sun because it was warn and he saw so little of it. He hated the snow and he hated Christmas. He hated the snow because he was thin and small and could not warm himself very well and he hated Christmas because nobody ever gave him a present or sent him a card.

He ran down the narrow stairs, his dog Boxer slipping down behind him. He looked at his plate of porridge on the table. It was grey and lumpy. He poured thin milk over it and began to eat. It did not taste very well but he had to be satisfied.

It was Boxer who first suggested that something unusual might have happened during the morning. He began jumping in the hall and scratching the front door.

"That dog will have to go one of these days," Missus Tucker said, giving him an angry look. "He had all my lawn torn up with his bones and he has almost worn a hole in the door from scraping it."

George Wallace opened the door and let Boxer out. But the dog did not run up the path as he usually did. Instead he kept barking for little George Wallace to follow him. George realised that something unusual was stirring and followed him.

He could not believe his eyes when he looked at the lawn. His eyes had often played tricks on him before when he was hungry but now they seemed to be playing the greatest trick of all. There in front of him, planted in the lawn, stood the largest and thickest lollipop he had ever seen. It was very large and very thick. He approached it with caution. Perhaps it was a mirage like he had heard about in the geography class. He remembered the lesson very well because it was about warm countries. He bent down and looked at it. It did not go away. Then he put out his index finger and felt the rim.

"Why its a real lollipop and quite as big and as thick as a plate. I wonder where it came from. I have never seen such a large lollipop in any of the shops."

Very gently he put his hands around the lollipop stick which was very thick also. He had to heave before the lollipop came away. He held it in front of him and looked at it with wide eyes. Then he gave it one long lick with all of his tongue. It tasted like a whole lot of sweet tastes blended together. There was raspberry there and blackberry and bilberry and strawberry too and many other tastes which he could not name. He licked for five minutes and then he was out of breath. Then he looked down and saw Boxer looking up at him with sad eyes. His tongue was panting and his tail was wagging.

"Why Boxer I have neglected you," he said and he felt very sorry for his little dog. So he bent down and pulled a small lollipop and held it in his free hand for the dog to lick.

Missus Tucker came to the door to see what was happening.

"George Wallace where did you get that lollipop?" she asked.

"It was growing in the garden."

"Lollipops don't grow in gardens."

"Well this one did and there are lots of others."

She came out and looked at them. She eyed them suspiciously.

"Sure they're not tainted?"

"No, they are the sweetest lollipops I ever tasted."

"Well I don't like it. I don't like it at all," she said and with that she turned and went indoors muttering to herself.

Little George Wallace had been given the pick of the lollipops. In other lawns in Hornbottom there were other lollipops but none to compare with the lollipop of little George Wallace. In one lawn there were no lollipops. Magus knew that Tony Drudges was a bully so he passed him by. Neither did he plant lollipops in Annabel Browne's garden. She was an only child and she was spoiled. Everthing she asked for had to be got immeditately or she would throw her temper and kick things. Magus had no time for such a child.

And now little George Wallace had a big problem. Should he bring the lollipop to school. If he did Tony Drudges might take it from him or it might fall and get broken. He decided against taking it to school. Instead he would leave it in his attic room and have a long lick from it each night before he went to bed. Already he had been licking it for a full twenty minutes and his tongue and mouth were sticky. But the lollipop was very long wearing which was the test of a good lollipop. And another strange thing about the lollipop, little George Wallace was warm for the first time in a very long time as if the lollipop contained not only the colours and tastes of all fruit but also the very warmth of the sun.

"What a way to start a day," he said to himself, too

happy to worry about school or say anything else. He put his large lollipop in his small room and took his school bag. On his way out he stopped and plucked some of the smaller lollipops and put them in his bag. He felt very happy walking up the sidewalk and every third step he took he jumped.

Everything would have gone well or at least better than it did before it finally went well had not Tommy Gloster been too greedy. The lollipop man had hesitated before he planted his lollipops in Tommy Gloster's garden and from a kind heart and against his better judgment he finally did so. He knew that Tommy was greedy. He had been sick from overeating during Christmas and now just before school he was sick again. He held his arms about his stomach and groaned with a terrible groan. Worse still, coloured spots came out on his face and his mother began to think he had been poisoned so she sent for Doctor Pink.

There was great excitement in the school yard. The children were comparing lollipops. Tony Drudges sulked in a corner and felt left out of things.

"Well George Wallace," somebody asked, "what type of lollipop did you get?"

"I got the largest lollipop of all."

"How big is it?" they asked.

"As big as a football and very thick. Why I licked it for a whole half hour this very morning and it just seemed as if I had never licked it at all."

"Fibber!" they all said.

"Its no fib."

"Well where is it then?"

"Got it at home. It is too large to bring to school."

"Well we've got to see it. Seeing is believing."

"Show it to you this evening but only from my top window just to prove to you that I have the biggest lollipop you have ever seen."

They felt that he was telling the truth and that made them jealous.

"Why should you have got the largest lollipop?" they asked.

"Don't know," he told them and that puzzled everybody.

The school was full of buzzes that morning. Whenever a teacher left the room there was a loud buzz of talk and when he turned to write on the blackboard there was a quieter buzz of talk. The teachers were angry and they called the headmaster. He was very tall and had gold rimmed glasses and when he peered down on children, as he did now, he made them feel very small.

"We must have silence," he told them. "And from what I hear there is a lot of whispering and talk going on. Has something or other happened?"

There was silence and nobody said anything. Then little George Wallace who had never spoken to the headmaster before put up his hand down at the end of the class room where he had been placed out of harm's way.

"Headmaster, a wonderful thing happened today, Lollipops have started to grow in Hornbottom."

"Foolish boy. Foolish boy. Lollipops don't grow in gardens or on trees for that matter. This is preposterous."

"But look sir! Look sir!" they all chanted and took out lollipops from their bags and shook the evidence at him, except of course Tony Drudges who was sullen and had nothing to show.

"Never heard such a thing in my life," the headmaster said. "Now settle down to your lessons and do not let me hear another word from you," and with that he left.

But they did not settle down. They whispered all day and bent their heads down behind the desks and licked their lollipops. They were made to stand in corners and face the wall and given lines to do but all to no avail. There was too much to buzz about.

Meanwhile Tommy Gloster was groaning more loudly than ever. The spots were getting larger and greener and redder and bluer. Doctor Pink arrived. He hummed and then he hawed and then he prodded Tommy Gloster in his very full tummy and told him that he should not gorge himself. But the doctor could not account for the large coloured spots. He had never learned from his large books that there were such things as lollipop blotches which came out all over the face when children like Tommy Gloster were too greedy.

Squire Wickle took a deep breath of Hornbottom air at the bottom of the hill. It was a beautiful summer day, a day for a friendly word here and a friendly word there and a cup of tea with the vicar who would not have the chimes of the clock fixed.

"Quite a strange fellow the vicar," he mused to himself as he stepped gingerly down the street. "Always reading old books and tinkering with machines. Odd. Distinctly odd. Never known him to turn up at the town hall for a meeting."

He looked about him. Yes, everything looked exactly like it had been yesterday. That was very satisfying.

It was all very satisfying until he arrived at Queen Street. He noticed Doctor' Pink's car parked outside the house of Missus Gloster.

"Wonder what all that can be about," he thought. He would go and see. So he crossed the road. Doctor Pink was emerging from Missus Gloster's house muttering something to himself.

"Strange, very strange, very very strange, Never seen anything quite like it before."

"What is so strange Doctor Pink?" Squire Wickle asked, overhearing the doctor.

"Master Gloster has come out in coloured spots. He has stuffed himself with lollipops and is quite ill. I have never seen spots like them before."

Squire Wickle was taken aback.

"Spots?" he asked.

"Yes."

"What type of spots."

"Large coloured spots."

"Oh goodness me! It is the plague again. I knew that this would happen sometime or other."

The milkman, Councillor Bitterberry, who had passed Magus the lollipopman early in the morning was just about to deliver Missus Gloster's milk when he heard the Squire mention the word plague.

"What did you say about plague Squire Wickle?" he asked.

"The plague has struck again," he told him with much agitation.

"And from what I can gather it is the plague of 1800."

"Well if that's so I'm delivering no milk to Missus Gloster. Don't wish to pick up any plague spots. Must have been that funny looking stranger I saw this morning behaving in a very curious manner. Going from garden to garden he was."

"A stranger?" the squire asked.

"Yes. Saw him this morning at seven o'clock and not a person stirring. Very odd he was with a long coat and a wide brimmed hat."

"Yes. He's the one who carried the plague to Hornbottom. I'm sure that he was the one."

"But I'm not sure that they are plague spots," Doctor Pink said.

"But you are *not* sure that they are *not* plague spots," the Squire said.

"Well that is true," the doctor said, a little confused at the manner in which Squire Wickle brought two negatives into his sentence.

"Fetch me a can of red paint. People must be warned," he told Councillor Bitterberry.

"Red paint?"

"Yes. You always put red paint on plague houses. That is what they did in 1800. Hornbottom must know that Missus Gloster and Tommy Gloster have the plague.

"You sure you know what you are doing?" Councillor Bitterberry asked.

"Of course I'm sure. We Wickles are sure of everything,"

Meanwhile Doctor Pink was stroking his chin. He too was very confused. He would have to look up his large medical books to find out exactly what was wrong with Tommy Gloster. In the meantime he would leave Squire Wickle to his ways. He knew that he was very strongheaded and once he got a notion into his head there was no changing it.

Councillor Bitterberry found a tin of paint and a brush. He brought it to Squire Wickle, who prized open the tin and mixed around the colouring until it was a strong equal red. Then with a brush dripping paint he approached Missus Gloster's door and drew a large cross upon it which bled red gouts of paint. Then he painted in bold and shivering letters on the wall the word PLAGUE.

"What are you doing to my door and wall?" Missus Gloster asked when she saw what was happening. "Why, it was only just before June that I had the painter come and paint my door and walls."

"Stay indoors. Stay indoors I beg of you. The plague has struck. Tommy Gloster has the plague."

"Well of all the nerve. My Tommy has not got the plague. Why, he's just got one of his tummyaches from eating one of those strange lollipops which he found in the garden this morning and he came out in spots."

"What lollipops?" the squire asked.

"Why the lollipops that were in all the gardens this

morning. If my Tommy has got the plague then all the children of Hornbottom must have the plague at this very moment."

"They are plague lollipops. That's what they are. Plague lollipops!" the squire cried. "We must summon all the councillors."

Now there was nothing the councillors of Hornbottom liked better than to be summoned, particularly in the case of an emergency, and this was an emergency. The last time they had been summoned in an emergency was on the occassion when an orange lorry had toppled over the parapet of the bridge and spilled its contents into the river. The children had followed the oranges downstream for miles and were lost for days in the woods. They were not the only people who were lost. The councillors went in search of them and they too got lost and had to be rescued by the children. But this had never been recorded in the council minutes.

The milkman was also the Hornbottom bell-man. He had a large bell in his milk float. He took the handbell and started to ring it.

"Hear ye! Hear ye!" he called, "The councillors of Hornbottom are summoned to the town hall to deal with the outbreak of red spotted plague."

He tolled the bell sadly and spoke his words in his deepest and darkest voice. No panic struck the town as he expected. No blinds were drawn. No shutters were drawn across windows and the town did not fall silent.

The councillors donned their red cloaks trimmed with rabbit fur and donned their councillors' hats, which they felt always made them wiser, and hurried to the town hall. Squire Wickle was there before them

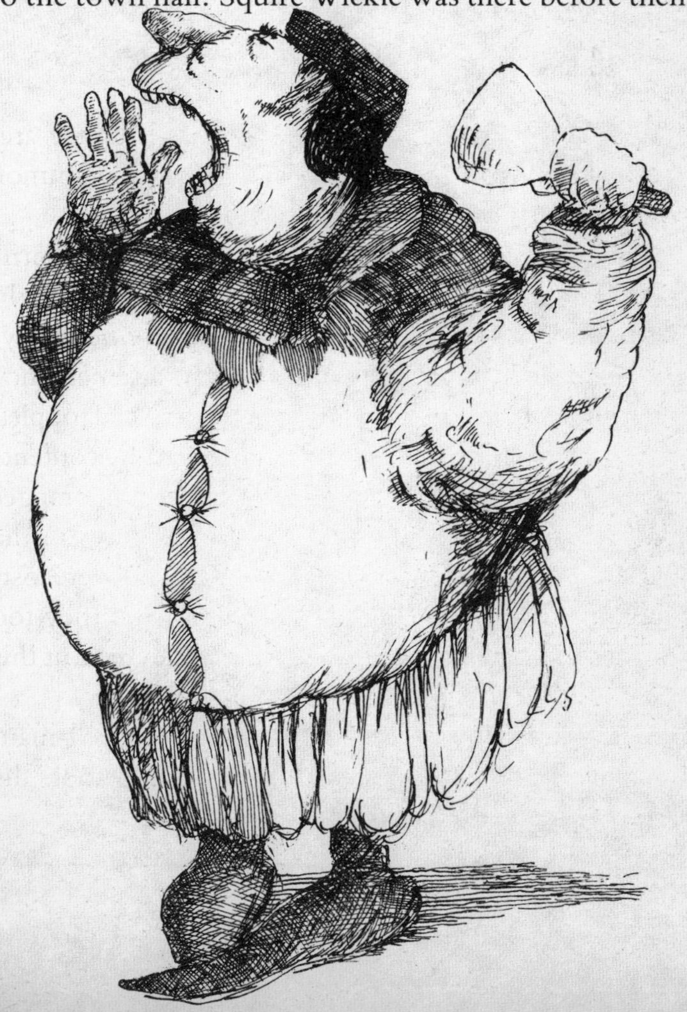

Harold Horse

seated on his large oak throne. When they had all taken their seats he took the gavel and crushed all talk. Then with his purple face and blue nose and great sense of his own importance he looked down upon them.

"Councillors," he began, "the plague has struck again."

"The plague of 1800?"

"The very same. Doctor Pink has identified the red plague spots on Tommy Gloster."

"Oh my! Oh my! What are we to do?"

"What are we to do but find this stranger who has planted plague lollipops in our midst and bring him to trial? We must find him and bring him here. If he carried the plague he must also carry the cure."

"Very wise. Very wise," they all said.

"What about the children?" Councillor Bitterberry asked. "We have forgotten the children. They have been eating lollipops all morning. We must go to the school."

They made a move to leave their seats.

"Stop!" Squire Wickle said. "If we do we might become tainted."

"Then what are we to do?" they asked.

"We must eat onions and garlic," Squire Wickle told them.

They all screwed up their faces at the thought. They hated onions and garlic.

"It is the only thing to do," Councillor Ridgeway said. He owned a vegetable shop and he thought that this was a very good way of getting rid of his onions and garlic. They took a vote amongst themselves and agreed that this was the wisest thing to do.

Councillor Ridgeway went to his shop and brought back a basket of onions and a basket of garlic. With horrid grins and funny grimaces the councillors ate the garlic and onions. Then, smelling very strongly, they left the town hall and made their way in the direction of the school. People held their noses when the councillors passed them. They were smelt at the school before they ever arrived there.

"What can I do for you?" the headmaster asked when he met them. He held a handkerchief in front of his nose.

"We have come to confiscate all lollipops, headmaster. They are plague lollipops and must be destroyed."

"What a day! What a day!" the headmaster said, directing Squire Wickle and the councillors to the main hall. "It has been a most distressing morning. Nothing but talk in the class rooms. The school smells like a jam factory."

He directed the councillors and Squire Wickle into the main hall and sat them around a large table on the stage to give them a sense of self importance and then he went and summoned all the pupils in the school.

From the stage the Squire could already see that the plague was spreading. There were definitely five children with large spots on their cheeks.

Squire Wickle came forward. He looked down at the rows of faces, looking for plague spots. He counted ten more faces with plague spots. The plague was speading before his eyes. He could also see children licking plague lollipops behind the backs of other children.

"I have come to collect your lollipops," he said. He tried to smile as if he were bringing the children good news. He had much to say but he never got the chance to say it. Suddenly there was a large "boo" from the centre of the hall which spread out to the sides and down to the front. It came up at the councillors and Squire Wickle in waves and on each wave came pellets of wet chewing gum and half licked lollipops and hard bits of paper shot from elastic bands.

"Steal our lollipops would you?" they cried. "Spoilsports. Nothing but old spoilsports. Same as you tried to take back the oranges from us before." And with that all the children were on their feet and moving towards the stage.

The councillors beat a hasty retreat and gathering their robes about them they hurried back panting very heavily to the town hall where they puffed and panted a lot before they regained their voices.

"We must capture the lollipop man! We must capture the lollipop man!" Squire Wickle told them. "And if needs be we will duck him in the ducking pond until we find the remedy for this plague."

"Agreed," they said.

"You fetch your guns and I will fetch my dogs," Squire Wickle told them, "we will track him down."

5

It was quite evident to Missus Perkins of the Yellow Tavern that the lollipops had done Master Barney Perkins a world of good. There was a healthy colour in his cheeks and he was laughing again. He had remained downstairs in the tavern and was sitting by the fire which Missus Perkins had lit for him. And Mister Perkins, the owner of the Tavern, could not believe his eyes.

"Why Barney," he said "I never seen you look so well in two years."

But Barney said nothing very much. He was too interested in licking his lollipops.

The patrons of the Yellow Tavern began to drift in at about six o' clock. The first man in was Harry the Ploughman. He had very broad shoulders and winter and summer he had the top button of his shirt open. He always tied his horse Betsy outside the tavern and gave her a bagfull of oats. She was a large quiet horse and she always carried Harry the Ploughman home at night time. He looked at Barney Perkins.

"Why, Master Barney, if you isn't all pinked up and healthy looking same as you was out with me in the fields all day. Swear you are not the same Barney

Perkins as I knew last week."

Barney Perkins smiled up at him. He liked Harry the Ploughman with his large hands and his wide shoulders which made the tavern roof look very low, and he liked his clog dance which he did on winter evenings to warm his feet.

"Heard all the rumpus down at the school, Mister Perkins?" he asked when he turned to take his pewter tankard of beer.

"Not a word."

"Councillors got one of those daft ideas of theirs. Say there is plague in the area. Squire Wickle fair gone soft in the head about it. Said it was due to some stranger who set lollipops in the gardens.

"Same lollipops as my Barney is eating?"

"Very same."

"Must be really gone soft in the head this time."

"Always felt that the councillors were soft."

"Haven't got a spark of sense between them."

"Really gone soft since they had those fancy dress coats of theirs made. You should have seen them run from the school. Tried to take the lollipops from the children. Said Tommy Gloster came out in spots. Children would have none of it. Like the Battle of Hastings it was up there."

"Never held with Squire Wickle," the tavern keeper said. "Why, he came in here once and tried to tell me how to run my tavern. Took the axe to him I did."

"Right and proper thing to do Mister Perkins. No call for people telling you how to run the Yellow Tavern."

"Right daft they are."

They fell silent for a moment and thought how daft the councillors were since they had had their fancy dress outfits made. It was a gentle summer evening and Harry the Ploughman talked and was silent and then talked again so that he would have something to say right through until it was closing time."

"Know something else," he said later, "Squire Wickle is getting out his hounds and the councillors are getting out their guns. They say that they are going to track down the lollipop man who brought the plague to Hornbottom."

Barney Perkins cocked his ears when he heard this. He would like to meet the Lollipop man who had planted the lollipops in front of the tavern. And now he was very disturbed when he heard that they were going to set Squire Wickle's dogs on him.

"You think they will catch the lollipop man Harry Ploughman?" he asked.

Harry the Ploughman looked down at him and knew that Barney Perkins was worried. He put his large thumb inside his leather belt, close to the iron buckle and said, "Master Barney, I've been asking myself the very same question. Thought I should warn the lollipop man. Then I fell to talking to myself and I said that if he could slip in and out of Hornbottom right under Squire Wickle's eye then he can outsmart those dogs. You see, Barney Perkins, the lollipop man is too wise and too long about to be captured by Squire Wickle. You mark my words."

"But you can't be sure Harry Ploughman. We got to go and warn him."

Their conversation was interrupted by the baying of

hounds. The lawn in front of the Yellow Tavern seemed to be filled with them barking and sniffing.

"You see Harry Ploughman we got to go and warn him. There is no knowing what those dogs will do to him."

Harry the Ploughman went to the window and looked out. He did not like what he saw. Squire Wickle's hounds were worrying his horse Betsy. The dogs were everywhere trying to pick up a scent. And the councillors were discharging guns up in the air to control the dogs and instead they were adding to the confusion. His horse Betsy had a frightened look in her eyes.

"Nobody is going to disturb my Betsy at her evening oats. Why, she's been working hard the whole day while Squire Wickle and the councillors were wasting their time up at the town hall."

With that he strode out through the door and strode into the centre of the confusion. He wrenched a double barrelled gun from one of the councillors and walked straight up to Squire Wickle.

"What's this? What this?" the Squire asked.

"This is a double barrelled gun Squire Wickle. You call off your dogs. They are worrying my Betsy."

"Why man, there is a plague in Hornbottom," the squire said.

"I know and I'm pointing a gun at it. Now I'm going to count to ten and I count fast. When I'm finished counting, you and your dogs and the fancy dress parade better be out of gun shot."

They knew better than to argue with Harry the Ploughman. They retreated down the road surrounded by barking dogs. Harry watched them go.

"They are in a bad mood," he thought. "I must find the lollipop man and give him a warning."

He walked back into the tavern. There was silence in the room. Everybody knew that Harry the Ploughman was in a very dark mood.

"Must warn the lollipop man," he told them, "no knowing what Squire Wickle and the councillors are up to."

"Will you take me with you Harry Ploughman?" pleaded Master Barney Perkins. "I would like to meet the lollipop man."

"You stop asking such things Barney Perkins," his mother told him. "You have not been out an evening since last year."

Harry the Ploughman looked at Barney Perkins. His eyes were full of pleading so he turned to Missus Perkins and said, "don't think there's anything wrong anymore with Barney Perkins. What he needs is a breath of summer air. You just wrap a blanket around him and I'll take him for a short ride on my horse

Betsy."

"You sure he will be alright Harry Ploughman?" Missus Perkins asked. Harry the Ploughman looked at her with his dark eyes and she knew that everthing would be all right. She could always depend on Harry the Ploughman.

She wrapped Barney Perkins in a blue blanket and Harry the Ploughman gathered him in his arms and carried him out of the door and set him on the front of his horse Betsy. Then he got up behind him.

He took the reins and they set out from the Yellow Tavern in search of the lollipop man. On their way down the road they saw little George Wallace coming towards them crying.

"Why are you crying George Wallace?" Harry the Ploughman asked.

"They are going to hurt the lollipop man. Only person in the town who was kind to me and they are going to hurt him. I hate Squire Wickle with his blue nose and his purple face," and having said that he started to cry again.

"Now George Wallace you get up here behind me and put your arms around me and we'll go in search of the lollipop man. Think I know where he might be."

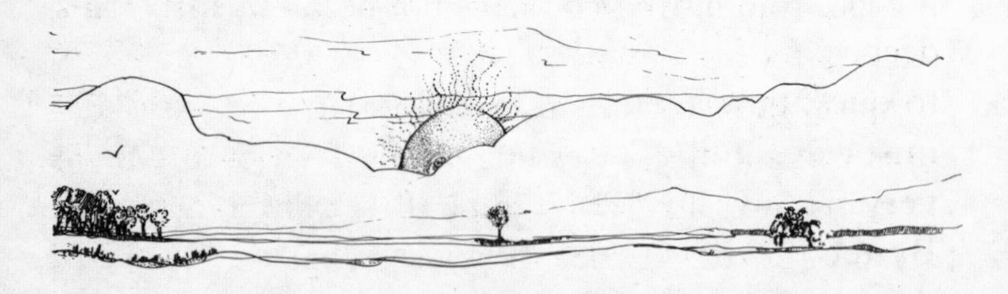

'You do?" they asked.

"Yes."

"Think Squire Wickle and the councillors will find him?" Barney Perkins asked.

"No."

"You sure of that?" little George Wallace asked.

"Quite sure."

The lollipop man had lain all day in the sun, his toes in warm shallow water. He was not very worried about Squire Wickle or the councillors. He had a good idea of what had been happening all day up at the town hall. By now he knew that the dogs would be following the lollipop trail he had set across the moors. That was the mistake Squire Wickle made. He did not know that dogs liked lollipops as well as children.

Squire Wickle and the councillors were by now following the dogs across the moor. The councillors were becoming tired and dirty and several of them had fallen into muddy pools and had to be rescued. And they seemed to be no way near to capturing the lollipop man.

"Forward! Forward!" Squire Wickle called, pointing deeper and deeper into the moors. They were beginning to question his wisdom. At eight o' clock, a summer mist rose up from the moor and thickened about them very rapidly. By nine o' clock they had lost the dogs. By ten they were cold and by eleven they knew that they were lost. They huddled together and kept themselves warm as best they could during the night.

Harry the Ploughman found the lollipop man down by the bank of the river as he suspected. He was snoring very loudly and happily when they came upon him and his large floppy hat was pulled over his eyes. Barny Perkins and little George Wallace stood and looked at him with their mouths open because they had never seen anybody quite like him before. After some time he opened one eye and looked up at them for a moment.

"Ah Barney Perkins and George Wallace. I see you have come to visit me. Did you like the lollipops I set in your lawns this very morning?" he asked.

"Oh yes," they said and they were going to say much more to him but they remembered why they had come to visit him.

"Oh Mister lollipop man, you better hurry away from here. You see Squire Wickle and the councillors are looking for you at this very moment. They do not like you at all and they have dogs and guns."

"Now Barney Perkins and George Wallace, you don't worry your small heads about the lollipop man. You see I have outwitted them. Do you know where they are at this very moment?"

"No."

"Why at this very moment they are out on the moor and very soon they will be lost."

"Why, you know everything lollipop man. You know our names and you know how to make lollipops we really like."

"Well, as a lollipop man gets old he learns lots of things. And I know two things. Firstly Barney Perkins is going to be strong and well again and secondly that you should be on your way back home again."

Lost on the moor

"And what about George Wallace, lollipop man?" Barney asked. "Why, he's always sad and miserable because he's an orphan."

The lollipop man looked at little George Wallace with his open eye. "You know what you are going to be when you grow up George Wallace?"

"No."

"Why, George Wallace, you are going to be a lollipop man just like me. There will be no lollipop man in England like George Wallace."

"You mean that, lollipop man?" whispered George.

"Yes, I mean that." And with that he closed his open eye.

"Now," he said, his eyes closed, "I'm going back to sleep again. You don't worry about the lollipop man. You go right back home to bed and get plenty of sleep and you look in your gardens again tomorrow morning. And thank you Harry Ploughman for bringing my two friends to visit me. Always like it when my friends call by."

And with that he started to snore and they felt that he wished to be left alone with his dreams. So Harry the Ploughman put them up on his horse Betsy and brought them home.

6

Next morning the lawns were full of lollipops again. They had doubled in number and their was great excitement among the children, except of course for Tony Drudges. The lollipop man never planted lollipops in the lawn of school bullies and he had no intention of making an exception of Tony Drudges.

"Why, I have never seen the children look so happy," Missus Perkins told Missus Gower at the food shop. "Little George Wallace is fleshing out and full of talk and my Barney is coming back to his old self again."

"Shame Squire Wickle and those councillors causing such a hue and cry. Why, you know something Missus Perkins, I think all those spots on Tommy Gloster came from over eating. Never known Tommy to leave off when he had enough. Why, he just stuffs himself. Always has. Remember last Christmas? Ate a whole pudding he did and came out in spots too."

"Squire Wickle is all hot and bothered about this plague."

"That's 'cause he's got nothing else to occupy his time. Why, he walks through the town at eleven each morning and you would swear that he owns the place."

The mothers of Hornbottom were in agreement on two things. Firstly that the lollipops were not plague carriers and secondly that the town was well rid of Squire Wickle and the councillors.

"Hope they stay away," the children said. "They are all spoilsports. Fancy trying to take our lollipops."

"Hope so to," the mothers told each other. "Always putting their noses in where they are not wanted. Never know what daft notion they are going to dream up next."

But the squire and the councillors did return. They returned without the dogs,. The dogs, running out of scent, had returned home and were yelping up at Wickle Hall. The squire and the councillors were wet and muddy and angry when they dragged themselves through the town. They felt distinct hostility from the people and some of them made bold to abuse them.

They knew that the lollipop man had led them a merry chase. They had decided upon that as they huddled together out on the dank moor. But they would get even with him. They would catch him and duck him in the ducking pond. They would leave no stone unturned and no corner unvisited until they came up with him.

Many of them had caught colds on the moors. They were chilled to the bones. They were angry. They would hide their anger for the moment but next morning, before sun up they would lie in wait for the lollipop man. Then they would pounce on him. He would answer to them for his actions.

When the councillors reached their homes there were no greetings for them. The children had carried the former day's happenings home from school and the mothers were none too pleased with the events. Clearly Squire Wickle had too much to say and very little to support what he said. And Constable Watkins was as bad as the councillors. All day he had paraded up and down, at a safe distance, before Missus Gloster's house, deaf to all her pleas.

"Got my orders Mum," he told her. "This house is suspected of harbouring the plague."

"But my Tommy's spots have all cleared up, Constable Watkins."

"I'm afraid that you must remain put Missus Gloster. These are my orders and I got to carry them out."

"Well I'm going right down to London to talk to the Prime Minister about this."

"Prime Minister has got nothing to do with it Missus Gloster. Squire Wickle and the councillors is Prime Minister in these parts."

And he swelled out his chest and felt very important. It was not every day he was called upon to parade before a plague house.

"Are you all right in there Missus Gloster?" the neighbours called from the pavement.

"No, I'm not. Why, its the same as if I were in the tower of London. Can't get any of my shopping done. And my Tommy is just crying out with hunger, the poor lamb."

"Must be all those lollipops he ate which brought out the spots," they said.

"Well you know my Tommy. He's a growing boy and has a large and healthy appetite."

"You sure its not too large and too healthy for your Tommy?" a neighbour asked.

Missus Gloster left the window. She felt insulted that anybody should suggest that her Tommy had over eaten. Why, he was just an ordinary boy, a little too fat perhaps, with a large and healthy appetite.

All day the councillors kept indoors or went about their business. They had decided not to show themselves more than they had to as it was quite evident to them that people had become hostile towards them in the last day. But in their minds they were spinning horrible plots as to what they would do with the lollipop man when they laid their hands upon him. He was lying in hiding somewhere but come the morning they knew that he would reappear to plant his lollipops. Then they would pounce.

Squire Wickle walked up and down the main hall of Wickle Hall the whole day. He was very angry. He had a score to settle. He had to meet up with the lollipop man and visit him with the harshest punishment of the law. Ah yes! He would see the lollipop man ducked in the ducking pond. Three times he would be ducked until he told Squire Wickle and the councillors the remedy for this plague in Hornbottom.

He was sitting in front of the large fire having his toddy when the ghost appeared and sat down opposite him. Squire Wickle looked at him in a very sour manner. The ghost did not seem terribly put out by his ill humour. He just rolled and chuckled and broke out in large bursts of laughter until the Squire thought he would take a turn and that would be the end of him. He would like to be rid of the meddlesome ghost once and for all.

"Saw you on the moor last night. My, did you look foolish floundering around in that muddy quagmire. Never saw anything quite like it for such a long time. Did me a world of good it did. Same as if somebody took a feather to my large toe."

"And you never lifted a finger to help us?"

"No, you did not merit any help. You have really grown to hate that lollipop man."

"He is carrying plague."

"Do you know what the plague really looks like?"

"No, but I've read all about it."

"Well, I do, and nobody has got the plague. The only people in Hornbottom who have the plague are Squire Wickle and his serious and sour councillors."

And then the ghost thought of them dragging themselves across the moor and he could not be serious any longer, so he rolled about in the armchair, binding his sides with his arms to protect himself from exploding with laughter.

"You are a dreadful ghost. Why the Wickles have always been well thought of in Hornbottom. They have made great contributions to this town."

"Yes, until you came along. Most of the Wickles were jolly men full of laughter. Why, Wickle Hall always echoed with laughter until you came along. And that statue of Grandfather Wickle in the square is not at all like the Grandfather Wickle I knew. He was not tall and thin. He was small and fat and bald and there was a Wickle twinkle in his eyes."

"You cannot have a statue of small, fat and bald men in public places. Lets the family down, that type of thing. Statues always strain the truth."

"I just cannot argue with you cousin, but things are going to change. Ah yes, things are going to change. But I must be on my way down to the main hall for a loud laugh. I never could laugh properly in an armchair."

And with that he went invisible and became visible in the large hall where he began to laugh anew.

Squire Wickle's face was very grim. The more he reflected on his futile track across the moors, the grimmer he became. He was losing his respect among

the councillors. They were grumbling and becoming rebellious. They laid the blame for their miseries at his feet. He had to come up with this lollipop man. He had a score to settle with him. And he was determined to settle it the very next morning.

7

It was a bright morning. The sun was pink and half hot when the lollipop man opened his eyes and looked at the world of dew-wet leaves and running water about him. He could pick out the different notes from the different birds right down the river bank. His large coat, which was very special, had kept him warm the whole night through. His old bones did not feel as stiff as they had felt the morning before.

He walked up along the river path his mind filled with the beauty of the morning and made his way over the humped bridge. He followed his usual route for setting the lollipops. He began at the Yellow Tavern which was set in a small open square. When he got into the narrow streets with the small gardens where the cold of the night still remained, he felt a chill which did not come from the cold of the night. He felt that eyes were upon him. He suddenly realised that there were figures in the alleyways. Before he could utter 'Jack Horner' they were upon him. They appeared from the dark shadowy places in their red councillors' robes. Leading them was Squire Wickle.

"Secure him well and keep a sharp eye on him. He is very wily and up to all sorts of tricks," Squire Wickle told them.

"He doesn't look very dangerous to me," one of the councillors said when they had secured him and put a pair of handcuffs on his hands.

"He's very old, Squire Wickle," another councillor said when they gathered around the lollipop man with his large floppy hat and his old face and grey beard.

"Ah, ha!" said the squire," He is full of all sorts of tricks. Why, I believe it was he who led us right across the moor and threw my dogs right off their scent. He must be ducked."

"No Squire, we had better bring him to the town hall and give him a hearing quickly before the people of Hornbottom know what we are about. This lollipop man has become very popular."

"Yes we must give him a trial," they all said.

The lollipop man was very quiet as he stood at the centre of all the bother. He had been in trouble before. A lollipop man had to expect this type of thing. There were some people who could not or would not understand and he was standing amongst them now.

They bundled the lollipop man off through the shadowy streets towards the town hall, Squire Wickle leading the way. The others dragged behind a little, not very enthusiastic at this early hour of the morning. In fact they were feeling distinctly foolish. Now that they had captured the lollipop man they were asking themselves what one did with a lollipop man who was old and kind looking and very inoffensive.

The capturing and securing of the lollipop man had not gone unnoticed. Little George Wallace had not slept very well that night, not because he was unhappy but because the lollipop man had said that he would become a famous lollipop man and also he had a hidden fear of what might happen if the old man were captured by Squire Wickle and the councillors. So he had twisted and turned all night and the sheets were all wound about him and his feet were popping out at the end of the bed. And because little George had not slept very well his little dog Boxer had not slept very well either. In fact it was the little dog who had warned him with a low growl that something was happening. He crept to the window and looked down. He was just in time to see the lollipop man being bundled off to the town hall.

"I have to tell somebody. I have to tell somebody about it," he told his dog. His dog understood and gave two little growls. The little dog did not like Squire Wickle or the councillors, particularly Councillor Bitterberry who had kicked him one day, not for any reason, but because he was little George Wallace's dog and nobody cared very much for little George Wallace. Not knowing what to do he bent his head down and began to cry. His little dog came and lay at his feet and curled up, one eye closed and one eye opened, looking at little George Wallace who was crying because the lollipop man had been captured.

And after he had cried for a little while he thought to himself that he should steal down to the town hall and see what was happening. He slipped down the stairs and out onto the street followed by his little dog. They crept into the town hall.

The lollipop man had been led into the council room and the councillors and Squire Wickle took their various important places. The lollipop man was left to stand in the centre of the room and the councillors and Squire Wickle were in positions where they could look down upon him. They felt a little awe in his presence for no reason that they could put their fingers upon. But not Squire Wickle.

"What is your name?" he called down from his oak throne.

"Magus," the lollipop man said.

"Magus what?"

"Just Magus."

"Where do you come from?"

"The borders of Wales."

"You practice magic then?"

"I suppose I do."

"Ah, I told you," said Squire Wickle jumping excitedly up from his large oak seat. "He is a magician. These magicians are dangerous fellows. Why, the punishment for practising magic is a ducking in the town pond. What type of magic do you deal in?"

"I make lollipops," Magus said and when the councillors heard that they rolled with laughter.

"He makes lollipops! He makes lollipops!" they said turning one to the other.

"Silence," cried the Squire, who did not take very kindly to laughter in the council chamber.

"There is nothing magical in making lollipops," one of the councillors called down at him. "Why, I could make lollipops if I set my mind to it."

The Lollipop man turned towards him and his eyes flashed in anger and the councillor who had made the remark stopped talking.

"There are many false lollipop men abroad. They do not know the old secrets as I do. They do not gather the right juices and berries at the right time. They do not make their colourings from the flowers and they do not gather honey from the honey combs. They make poor imitations of lollipops. The true lollipops carry all the tastes and colours of nature."

"Tosh and piffle. Tosh and piffle." Squire Wickle called down. "There are no such secrets. You are a dangerous man and you trifle with the secrets of nature. You carry a plague about in your pockets."

The Lollipop man looked up at Squire Wickle with blazing eyes. "You are a sour man Squire Wickle and you want all life about you to be sour. You are a disgrace to the Wickles. I remember your grandfather. You do not like to be reminded of your grandfather who made lollipops. He was one of the great lollipop makers."

Squire Wickle's face became intensely purple. Clearly this Magus fellow knew more than was good for him.

"No Wickles ever made lollipops. There is no record of a Wickle making ridiculous lollipops."

"I know," said the lollipop man." Things like that are not written in records. And the secret lollipop kitchens have been bricked up for forty years at Wickle Hall. I know because I learned how to make lollipops from your grandfather in the cellars of Wickle Hall."

"Is this true Squire Wickle?" the councillors asked.

"Tosh and piffle. Tosh and piffle. Can you imagine a

Wickle making lollipops?" the Squire said, not answering the question.

The lollipop man looked at him and continued. "And what of the ghost which haunts Wickle Hall? Why, he is the happiest ghost in all England. He was the ancestor who received Wickle Hall from the king."

The councillors were getting uneasy in their seats. Clearly Magus the lollipop man was much more than they had bargained for. He knew too much. If he could tell Squire Wickle so much about his ancestors he might be able to tell them much about themselves which they would not like to hear. He might tell the butcher that his weights were false and the milkman that his milk was watered down or the baker that his flour was weak. He was most dangerous, this lollipop man. He would have to get a ducking in the town pond.

"He will have to be ducked," they all called. "He will have to be ducked at twelve o'clock when all the children are at school. In the meantime he must be locked in the town hall cellar."

"All agreed?" Squire Wickle asked.

"All agreed," they said.

8

And that was enough for little George Wallace and his dog Boxer. He ran from the town hall and he kept running, followed by his little dog, until he arrived at Harry the Ploughman's cottage which was down by the river and a little away from everybody else. Harry was having his breakfast of brown bread, red cheese and strong tea when he rushed into the kitchen. Gasping for breath he told him about all that he had seen and all that he had heard.

"You mean to say that Squire Wickle has secrets locked away in the cellars of Wickle Hall?" Harry the Ploughman asked.

"Yes. That's what the lollipop man said."

Harry the Ploughman mused for awhile.

"You did the right thing coming to me George Wallace. They are afraid of what the lollipop man could tell them. But they do not know that the lollipop man has friends in Harry Ploughman and George Wallace. We got to make our plans you and I."

Harry fetched another mug and poured little George Wallace some of his strong tea and buttered some brown bread for him. Then they sat and talked for a while and made their plans.

"Now, you go to school, same as nothing has happened and you know what you have to tell the children in the school. And tell them Harry Ploughman sent you."

"I'll do that Harry Ploughman," he said.

Little George Wallace went home and collected his school bag and made his way up to the school playground. He gathered some of the children about him and explained exactly what had happened during the morning from the moment he lifted the corner of the curtain in his room.

After little George Wallace told them what had happened, the children began to grumble and be angry. More children gathered about little George Wallace.

"Saw the councillors and Squire Wickle coming out of the town hall this morning," Bill Hutton said. "They really looked in a dark mood as if they had sentenced somebody to the gallows. They have been behaving most peculiarly for the last few days ever since Squire Wickle got the daft notion that there was plague in the town. Why, my gran said that it wasn't plague. It just came from people eating too many lollipops and she ought to know because she is so old."

"I've been and listened," little George Wallace said. "They are going to duck the lollipop man in the pond at twelve o'clock. They said that twelve o'clock was the best time because there would be nobody around and the children would be up at the school."

"Well they have something else coming to them. Why, they are about as mean as anybody when they would duck a lollipop man in the pond. Wonder how Squire Wickle would like to be ducked and come up all all wet and covered with green slime and his pockets full of tadpoles?" Bill Hutton asked.

"Yes how would he like that?" they all asked.

"Well that's what Harry Ploughman wishes to know too," little George Wallace said.

"What does Harry Ploughman wish us to do?"

"I'll tell you," little George Wallace said, and when they gathered about him he told them.

And that morning the headmaster was very pleased with the children. He had never known the school to be so quiet. In fact it was too quiet.

"Well at least all this bother with the lollipops is over," he told his teachers when they were having tea at the eleven o'clock break. If he had listened closely he might have noticed that the noise coming from the school yard was from the smaller pupils. They had been given orders to make as much noise as possible so as to give the impression that the school yard was full.

As for the rest of the pupils, they had melted away like the snow. Some had slipped through the main gates, others had crawled through the small hole in the timber fence at the back of the school and many had climbed over the school wall. They all made their way to the small wood beside the ducking pond armed with ripe tomatoes, rotten oranges and whatever else they could filch from the dustbins along the way. Harry the Ploughman was waiting for them in the wood smoking his pipe, his horse Betsy tied to a tree.

When they had gathered around him in the tall summer grass he said, "When I charge with Betsy you charge after me. Do not move until you see me leap on Betsy' back."

He arranged them in ordered lines and told them to place their missiles in front of them on the ground.

"It must be a complete surprise. Our object is to free Magus the lollipop man and capture Squire Wickle. We'll give him a taste of his own medicine, won't we boys?"

"Yes, Harry Ploughman! We'll give him a taste of his own medicine," they all cried and looked at their ripe tomatoes and rotten oranges more closely. Yes, they were just the oranges and tomatoes to deal with the Squire and the councillors. They were good and mashy. No use throwing them unless they were good and mashy.

At twelve o' clock, the church bells chimed thirteen times. The councillors and Squire Wickle, dressed in their robes in order to lend pomp to the mean occasion, brought Magus the Lollipop man across the village green to the ducking pond. Harry Ploughman and the children observed the happenings from the high grass. Squire Wickle unrolled a parchment he had in his hand and read out accusations against Magus in old English which Harry Ploughman did not understand very well. And while the accusations were being read Magus the lollipop man stood quite still and unfussed. The councillors began to fidget among themselves while Squire Wickle read from the parchment.

"Let's get it over with," they cried and with that they carried the lollipop man to the large old ducking chair and secured him to its oak arms.

"Out with it now," they called, "and give him a proper ducking. That will teach him to keep his secrets to himself,"

They caught the shaft of the ducking chair and were about to pull it around and whirl the lollipop man out over the pool when Harry Ploughman leaped on Betsy's back. He brandished his knobbed stick and cried. "CHARGE!"

And up from the long grass in the small wood rose the children of Hornbottom and little George Wallace's dog Boxer and charged row by row in perfect order as Harry Ploughman had told them. Harry Ploughman's horse Betsy thundered across the green kicking up tufts of lawn with its large shoes and Harry Ploughman swirling his knobbed stick above his head. He charged among the councillors and brought the stick down on their heads and backs. And while they nursed bumps on their heads they were showered with over-ripe tomatoes and rotten oranges and some stale eggs which exploded with horrible smells. And little George Wallace's dog Boxer seemed to be everywhere, biting at shins and tearing at councillors' robes.

"Serves them right," some of the women of Hornbottom said who had gathered to see the goings on.

The councillors fled for the second time in two days. Across the town green they fled pursued by angry children. Meanwhile at the ducking chair fortunes had suddenly changed for the worse for Squire Wickle. He was pinned to the ground by several children while

others led by little George Wallace set Magus the lollipop man free.

"That was a near thing Mister Lollipop man," they told him. "Another minute and you would have had a right ducking."

"Never feared for a moment," Magus the lollipop man said in a deep calm voice. "Why, down in my very toes I knew that help was on its way. Something told me, which tells me everything, that George Wallace and Harry Ploughman had everything under control"

Harry Ploughman strapped Squire Wickle into the ducking chair. Then he caught the long beam of the ducking chair and brought it around until Squire Wickle was above the centre of the pond and below him was the thick green slime and millions of tadpoles; black blobs with black tails.

"Mercy! Mercy!" the Squire called.

But he had no time to call for mercy a third time. Harry Ploughman heaved up the beam and down went the chair with Squire Wickle. He was under the pond surface for a whole two seconds and when Harry Ploughman brought him up again his head was covered with a wig of green pond slime, and water alive with tadpoles was running from his pockets.

"Mercy, mercy!" he cried, "I have done wrong. I

have done wrong. I have deprived the children of Hornbottom of their lollipops. I have tried to drive the lollipop man from the town."

Harry Ploughman was going to duck him once more but Magus the Lollipop man said, "Enough. Enough. He has learned his lesson. I do not think he will be ever quite the same again. So bring him. I have some words to say to him."

Harry Ploughman brought him in. And while he was bringing him in the children gathered about the lollipop man and gazed up at him in amazement. He looked exactly what a lollipop man should be like with his floppy hat with its large brim and his huge overcoat.

"And now I must reward my friends," he said plunging his hands deep into his pockets. He drew out large handfuls of lollipops and let the children choose their favourite colours. And when they had taken all the lollipops he had in his hands he plunged down and drew out some more. The children decided that they were magical pockets with no bottoms.

Squire Wickle was a very sorry sight when he was brought before Magus the lollipop man. He knew that his power had gone forever. He would never again sit in his large oak throne in the town hall and nobody would ever listen to him again.

"I have something to say to you Squire Wickle. You have done me wrong and for a very long time you have done yourself wrong. Well you know the secrets of Wickle Hall and well you know that the Wickles have made lollipops for the children of this whole county for longer than we lollipop makers can remember. Why the Wickles made the best lollipops ever licked in Merry England. Is that not true?"

"Yes, that is true," Squire Wickle said, his head hanging down in shame.

"And you still know the secrets which your grandfather told you? Why he knew all the secrets. Had I not come by here, why, all the old secrets might have perished. And that would be very sad indeed."

"That is true," the Squire said, "but making lollipops is not a very serious business."

"Ah! That is the mistake you made. Making lollipops is the most serious business in the world. Why, an imposter could have taken over and children might never have known the true taste of lollipops."

"Its a very serious business making lollipops," the children told him.

"Is it?" the Squire asked.

"Much more important than being a councillor," the lollipop man said.

"Do you think so?" the Squire asked.

"I have always thought so. I have always thought so. There would be no more happiness in the world if lollipop men forgot the old secrets."

"Then let us go back to Wickle Hall and break down the bricks which have hidden the lollipop cellars for far too long," the Squire said, enthusiasm which he had long thought dead, coming back to him.

They were all eager to march on Wickle Hall and break down the walls which concealed the cellars but Magus put up his large hands.

"No. I am afraid that we cannot do that. Lollipop making is a very private thing. Its secrets must be kept very closely. Only four are permitted to return to Wickle Hall, Squire Wickle, Harry Ploughman, George Wallace and myself."

There were many sad faces amongst the children.

"I wish you to return to school and make a promise to me that you will never tell anybody the secrets of Wickle Hall," the lollipop man said.

"We promise," they said.

"Good. You have saved the day and I will never forget the help you have given me. Now return quietly to school."

They all returned to school rather sadly, all of course except Little George Wallace who would become the greatest lollipop maker in all England.

Little George Wallace would not be missed at school. He never was because he was so small and so unimportant.

9

The four of them and little George Wallace's dog Boxer made their way back to Wickle Hall and when Squire Wickle was washed and dry Harry Ploughman got a large sledge hammer. They went down to the cellars and Squire Wickle pointed to an old wall which was grey with dust and cobwebs. Harry Ploughman flexed his muscles, took the sledge hammer, swung it about and brought it down heavily against the wall. The wall crumbled easily and when Harry Ploughman finished his work they lit lanterns and made their way into the hidden lollipop kitchens. The kitchens lay exactly as they had lain when Squire Wickle had bricked them up as a young man.

On shelves stood large coloured bottles with long narrow shapes and round bulbous shapes and all sorts of other shapes that were very hard to describe. And there were copper cauldrons everywhere which were large and deep and wide and hugh wooden spoons for mixing the sugars and juices.

Magus was taken aback and stifled a tear, "Why, it was right here that I learned my trade and me just a boy like George Wallace here. There is no lollipop kitchen like it in all England."

"Nothing has changed," the Squire said, "I was very foolish shutting off this wonderful world. I was always happy here, but I thought it beneath a Wickle to make lollipops."

"Look at all the years you have wasted," Magus said.

"Well, we've got to start again. All those bottles have to be filled. Now is the time for gathering berries and pressing out the juices," Squire Wickle said.

"That is correct," said Magus "We will have to gather the juices now during the long days and press them and fill up the bottles. In the winter time you can boil them all together with honey and syrup. Think you have forgotten the old secrets?"

"No. They may be a bit rusty but I have not forgotten them. It is in the Wickle blood to make lollipops and we do not forget easily."

"Are you quite sure of that?"

"Yes."

"Good, I was worried for a while. But I will stay with you until autumn and help you gather and crush the berries."

That night Magus and Squire Wickle sat about the fire and talked about the old secrets of lollipop making. Squire Wickle's fingers were all sticky with juice and honey and they were sticking to his toddy glass. But he had never been happier in his life now that his secret had been discovered. A little after midnight the ghost appeared. He was very sad. He looked into the fire and said nothing.

"This is an ancestor of mine," Squire Wickle said. "He was jester to the king in London many hundreds of years ago. You have heard of him. He is a laughing ghost."

"I'm pleased to meet you," Magus said looking over at him. The ghost was sniffling.

"Something troubling him?" Magus said.

"Something troubling you, ancestor?" Squire Wickle asked.

"Yes," he answered "My haunting days in this house are over. I have to leave now that you are going to make lollipops again. You see Wickle Hall in the past always rang with laughter and I was sent back to keep up the tradition. Now I have to leave because you have changed so much. I will be most unhappy leaving the place."

"This is indeed a very serious matter, ancestor," Squire Wickle said.

"I know," the ghost replied.

They were all very thoughtful about the fire. There must be some way out of the difficulty, they thought to themselves.

"Seems to me we might be able to get around the problem," Magus said. "You see Squire Wickle has been so serious for such a long time that he has forgotten how to laugh and it will take a very long time for him to recover. I think that would allow you to stay around for a very long time."

"Think the ghosts would accept that?" asked the ghost looking a little more cheerful.

"I think they might," said Magus. "Ghosts understand arguments like that, but I think that you have a confession to make about George Wallace."

"Yes. I must say that I have been dishonest. I have kept a secret from you cousin," said the ghost.

"You have?"

"Yes. You see George Wallace is one of us. You remember when cousin Angus from Scotland was drowned off Cornwall with his young son some years ago."

"Yes. Both were lost."

"No. Only Cousin Angus was lost. The child was washed up much further down the coast. Nobody knew where he came from. Well, that child is George Wallace. You will find the Wickle birth mark on his arm."

Squire Wickle was very amazed at the news. He was happy when he thought about it. The secret of lollipop making would stay in the Wickle family.

"I will bring him straight to Wickle Hall tomorrow," said the Squire. Why, Missus Tucker has treated him very poorly since he was brought to Hornbottom."

And that was how George Wallace was brought to live in Wickle Hall. He was given a pony for himself and the local carpenter made a kennel for his small dog Boxer. And every evening after school he took his pony and went in search of berries on the Wickle lands.

A whole four months Squire Wickle, Magus and George-Wallace spent gathering honey and juices and boiling syrups until the bottles in the cellar were all filled again and the syrup cauldrons filled with thick syrups. The whole house smelt like the fields in autumn and the smells would last right through the winter until they were locked away in lollipops.

Then one evening when the sun was full of gold and the sky full of honey, the lollipop man said it was time for him to go. He would have to get back to his own lollipop kitchens. The squire and little George Wallace went with him down the avenue to the iron gates. They were sad that he had to leave. But then children somewhere or other would be without lollipops if he did not go. They shook hands and he passed out through the gates. They watched him go down the hill with his floppy hat and his large overcoat and his careful slow walk.